This igloo book belongs to:

....

Contents

igloobooks

Published in 2016
by Igloo Books Ltd
Cottage Farm
Sywell
NN6 0BJ
www.igloobooks.com

LEO002 0616
10 9 8 7 6 5 4 3 2
ISBN: 978-1-78440-176-4

Illustrated by Diane Le Feyer

Printed and manufactured in China

My 6-in-1 Treasury

The Ugly Duckling
and other
Fairytales

igloobooks

The Little Mermaid

Once, a little mermaid wanted to see the world above the sea. So, she said goodbye to her sisters and her father and swam to the surface. There, she saw a prince standing on the deck of a royal ship.

The little mermaid fell in love with the prince. She was about to call out to him when suddenly, a great storm blew. Lightning flashed and thunder crashed and the ship began to sink. "I must rescue the prince," gasped the little mermaid.

The little mermaid pulled the prince ashore. She watched until a girl found him. When the prince woke, he thought the girl had rescued him. "I wish I could walk on land," said the little mermaid, diving below the waves.

In the deep ocean, the little mermaid found the sea witch. "I will give you legs so that you can walk," said the witch, "but in return, I will take your voice."

The little mermaid agreed and as she swam upwards, her tail became two legs.

The little mermaid went to the prince's palace.
The prince felt sorry for this girl who could not speak
and treated her like his own sister. As time passed,
the little mermaid fell more in love with him.

One day, the prince said that the king and queen had commanded him to marry another princess. When he met the princess, the prince realised it was the girl who had found him on the beach. He fell instantly in love and the two were married.

The heartbroken little mermaid dived back into the sea. Her legs became a tail and she swam to her sisters who waited nearby. "Do not cry, sister," they said, "for you belong with us, beneath the sea."

The prince never saw the little mermaid again. However, on fine days, when the sun shimmered on the water, he imagined he saw the flick of a golden tail before it disappeared, down, down, into the deep, blue ocean.

The Ugly Duckling

In the country, near a sleepy farm, a mother duck sat on her nest of eggs. One after another, the eggs cracked open and the ducklings hatched.

Just one, very large, egg was left. Suddenly, there was a cracking sound. A fluffy head poked out, then a body. The mother duck stared and stared. This duckling was not at all like the others. It was big, grey and ugly.

In the farmyard, the animals stared at the mother duck's latest arrival. "What an ugly duckling!" they all cried. The poor little duckling was pecked and chased. So, he ran away from the farm as fast as his legs could carry him.

The duckling came to a cottage where an old woman lived with a hen and a cat. "If you cluck and hiss like us, you can stay," said the hen and cat.

The ugly duckling could not hiss or cluck, so he left the cottage.

Winter came and the little duckling was all alone.
The reeds and river froze and he was trapped by ice
and snow. Luckily for him, a man was passing by.
He pulled the shivering duckling from the ice and
took him home.

The man's children were very excited. They wanted to play with the duckling, but he flapped his wings in fright and he knocked things over. "Stop! Stop!" screeched the man's wife. The terrified duckling ran out through the open door into the snow.

The little duckling suffered so much during that long winter until the first spring sunshine came. The duckling flapped his wings and suddenly realised that he was flying! He flew across the fields, down to a lake where three elegant birds swam.

The ugly duckling bowed his head and, in the rippling water, he saw his own reflection. It wasn't that of a grey, ugly duckling, but a graceful swan. At last he had found where he belonged. Never again would the swan be seen as the ugly duckling.

The Elves and the Shoemaker

Long ago, a poor shoemaker had only enough leather left for one pair of shoes. "If I do not make and sell the shoes tomorrow," he said, "we shall surely starve." With that, the worried shoemaker and his wife went to bed.

The next morning, to his complete amazement, the shoemaker found a wonderful pair of shoes on his workbench. The stitching was the finest he had ever seen. The astonished shoemaker put the shoes in the window of the shop and they sold immediately.

Each night after that, the shoemaker would leave leather on the workbench. Each morning, there would be another beautiful pair of shoes. News spread of the shoemaker and wealthy people from far and wide came to buy the shoes.

The shoemaker had enough money to buy the finest leather in the land. Even more people came to buy the beautiful shoes and soon the shoemaker and his wife became rich. They both wished they knew who had brought them such good fortune.

That night, the shoemaker and his wife hid.
Soon, they saw two elves jump up on the workbench
and begin to make more fine shoes. "Their clothes
are so very ragged," whispered the shoemaker's wife.
"I shall make them some new ones."

The shoemaker got his finest leather and made tiny boots and shoes. His wife stitched little suits and caps, edged with gold thread. The shoemaker and his wife cut and shaped and stitched and sewed until the outfits were complete.

That night, just before the clock struck midnight, the shoemaker and his wife left the new clothes on the workbench. Then, they hid behind the curtain and waited. Very soon, the elves jumped up onto the workbench and saw the suits, caps, shoes and boots.

The elves put on the clothes and danced with joy. Then, they left the shop and never came back. The shoemaker and his wife did not mind. They would always be grateful to the little elves who had made their fortune.

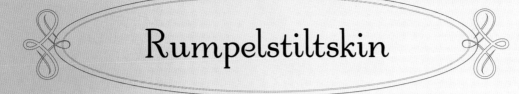

Rumpelstiltskin

Once, a miller boasted to a king that his daughter could turn straw into gold. "Turn this straw into gold or I'll lock you in the dungeon," said the king to the girl. The poor girl sat down at the spinning wheel and felt very frightened.

Just then, a little man appeared. He was all dressed in green and had red hair and a beard. "What will you give me if I do it for you?" he asked. The girl held out her necklace and the little man set to work.

By morning, the straw had been spun into gold and the little man disappeared. When the king arrived, he could not believe his eyes, but he was greedy and wanted more gold. So, he took the girl to a larger room full of straw.

Once again, the little man appeared, but this time the miller's daughter had nothing to give him. "Then, you must give me your first child," said the strange little man and the girl agreed. So, the straw was spun to gold and the king was so delighted, he asked the girl to marry him.

Some years later, the queen had a baby girl. She had forgotten all about her promise to the strange man, until one day he suddenly appeared. "Please don't take my child," she begged.

"Guess my name and you may keep your child," said the little man.

So, the queen sent royal servants to gather every name in the land. When the man appeared again, the queen read all the names out. "No, that is not my name," said the man to each one in turn and he left.

That night, high in the mountains, a servant was returning to the palace. Suddenly, he saw a little man dancing and singing, "No one else can guess my game that Rumpelstiltskin is my name."

"I must tell the queen," said the servant.

The next day, the little man came to take the baby.
"Rumpelstiltskin is your name!" cried the queen.
The little man was so angry, he jumped up and down
and disappeared in a puff of smoke and no one ever
saw Rumpelstiltskin again.

The Twelve Dancing Princesses

Once, a king had twelve daughters. At night, the king locked the princesses' bedroom door to keep them safe. However, each morning their shoes were worn through and full of holes. "This mystery must be solved," said the king.

The king summoned princes from all over the land. They all tried to find out where the princesses went, but each one failed. The king wondered if he would ever find the answer to the riddle.

Then, one day, a soldier was travelling through the kingdom when he met a mysterious old woman. She told him about the princesses. "If you want to solve the riddle, pretend to fall asleep and wear this magic cloak," she said.

The soldier went to the palace and pretended to fall asleep. The princesses changed into their beautiful ballgowns and dancing shoes, then they disappeared down a secret trap door. The soldier slipped on his magical cloak and followed them, unseen.

The princesses went through a forest of silver trees and the soldier broke off a glimmering branch with a snap. As the princesses went through forests of gold and diamonds, the youngest princess heard the same snapping sound, but she could see nothing.

At last they came to a lake, where twelve princes in twelve enchanted boats took the princesses to a magical, glittering castle. The soldier climbed into the last princess's boat. "How strange," said the prince who was rowing. "The boat seems heavier than usual."

Inside the castle, the princesses danced with the princes all night long.

When the time came for them to go home, the princesses went across the lake, through the trees of diamonds, silver and gold and back to their beds in the palace.

The next morning, the soldier told the king about
the princesses and showed him the branches.
At last the mystery was solved. "You may marry
my youngest daughter," said the happy king.

So, the soldier and the youngest princess married
and everyone lived happily ever after.

Tom Thumb

Once a poor man and woman had a baby boy who grew to be no bigger than a thumb. They called him Tom Thumb and each day he would sit by the ear of their carthorse as his father went off to cut wood.

One day, two men saw the tiny boy and offered the man a bag of gold. "We could make our fortune showing him to people in the city," they said.

"Let me go, Papa," said Tom, "I promise that I shall return."

Tom went with the two men, but when they stopped for a rest, he escaped into a mouse hole. When night fell, he crept into an empty snail shell and was just about to fall asleep when he heard the men talking.

"Let's rob that house we passed earlier," they said.
"I can crawl under the door!" cried Tom, jumping out
of the snail shell.

The two men agreed and took Tom along, so he
could crawl under the door.

Inside the house, Tom shouted so loudly, the robbers ran away. The house owner was so grateful to Tom, he gave him a big bag of gold.

So, clever Tom Thumb took the gold home and he and his parents were never poor again.